BENJE

THE SQUIRREL WHO LOST HIS TAIL

Written and
illustrated by
ELIZABETH RICE

 CHILDRENS PRESS, CHICAGO

TO MAE and EDDIE

Library of Congress Catalog Card Number: 79-82115

5 6 7 8 9 10 11 12 13 14 15 16 17 18 19 20 21 22 23 24 25   R   75 74

"Why are you crying, Benje?"

"Last night I was dragging my tail along the ground. It got caught in a trap, and I lost most of it. Oh, my beautiful tail!"

Soon Benje's other friends
heard the news. They tried to
make Benje a new tail.

It would not stay on, and
Benje cried again.

The other squirrels asked him
to come and play.

But Benje would only sit
and look sad.
All his friends had tails.

The raccoon.

The opossum.

The skunk.

And all the other squirrels.

Only he, Benje, was different.

After a while, since Benje
only sat and cried, his friends
left him alone.

One day Benje went down to
the river and sat on an old log.

While he sat there, feeling
sorry for himself, a bullfrog
plopped down beside him.

"Why so sad?" asked the
bullfrog.

Benje told him his sad story.
"Who needs a tail?" croaked
the bullfrog. "I had one once
and lost it. Good riddance, too!"

"Many animals have no tails
to speak of," said the bullfrog.

"Little cottontail is happy
with just a fluff of a tail."

"And the deer."

Benje was still unhappy. When
he began to cry again, the bullfrog
jumped into the river and swam away.

As the days passed, Benje
became more and more unhappy.

Late one evening, a barn owl
lit in Benje's tree.

"Why so sad?" asked the owl.

"I'm not like other squirrels," cried Benje. "I do not have enough tail to swish.

"Sometimes, I lose my balance. I fall when I jump from limb to limb."

The wise old owl blinked his eyes and said, "Benje, sometimes things happen, and you must learn to make the best of it. Learn to get along with what you have. Spread your feet for balance when you jump."

The owl and Benje talked far into the night.
Benje thought about what the owl told him.

The next
morning
he practiced
running
up and down
the tree.

He tried jumping
from limb to limb. And he
found that, with practice, he could
do all the things he could do before,
except swish his tail. But that really
was not very important.

That is how Benje learned to get along with what he had. He was happy again, and all his friends were happy, too.